Once you shop...You can't stop!

THE ULTIMATE COLLECTOR'S GUIDE
by Jenne Simon

  SCHOLASTIC INC.

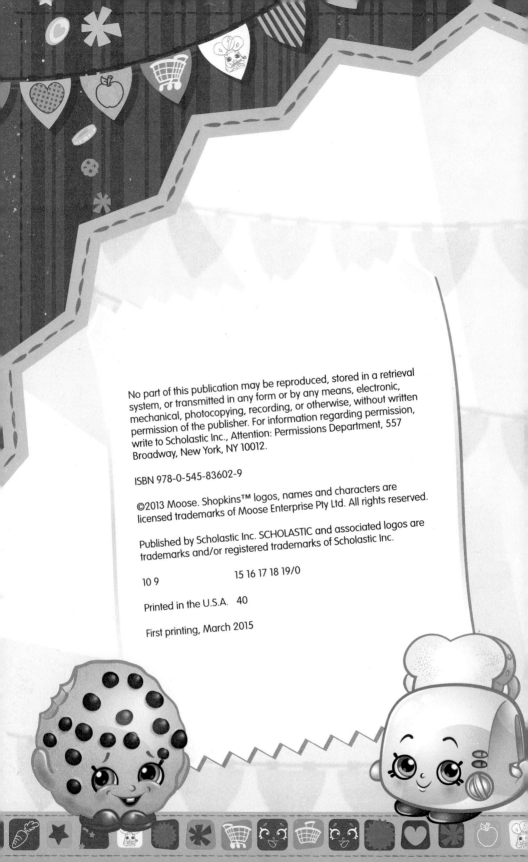

ISBN 978-0-545-83602-9

©2013 Moose. Shopkins™ logos, names and characters are licensed trademarks of Moose Enterprise Pty Ltd. All rights reserved.

Published by Scholastic Inc. SCHOLASTIC and associated logos are trademarks and/or registered trademarks of Scholastic Inc.

10 9   15 16 17 18 19/0

Printed in the U.S.A.   40

First printing, March 2015

TABLE OF CONTENTS

Welcome to Small Mart, the home of all your favorite Shopkins™! Grab your cart and head down each aisle to learn about Apple Blossom, Chee Zee, Cheeky Chocolate, Strawberry Kiss, and their friends. There's a world of fun in store, and it's time to start shopping. Check you later!

The Fruit and Veg aisle is the perfect place to play! The Shopkins who hang out here are bursting with personality, and there isn't a bad apple in the bunch!

FRUIT & VEG

APPLE BLOSSOM

FAVORITE COLOR:
Granny Smith green

PERSONALITY:
Sweet, tart, and a bit saucy

SIGNATURE DANCE MOVE:
The worm

FAVORITE VACATION DESTINATION:
Mount Fuji

FAVORITE WEATHER:
A crisp fall day

FIRST MEMORY:
Sprouting from just a wee, little seed

QUOTE:
"Check me out!"

At her core, Apple Blossom is sweet as pie and always up for adventure—she's ready to take a bite out of life!

★★★★★ CHLOE FLOWER ★★★★★★

HOBBY:
Leafing through the newspaper

BAD HABIT:
Stalking out of a room
when she's angry

BEST FRIEND:
Rockin' Broc

PERSONAL HERO:
Florets Nightingale

QUOTE:
"Let's veg out!"

★★★ MISS MUSHY-MOO ★★★★★

LIKES:
Dark, damp places

HOBBY:
Dirt-bike racing and making mud pies

FAVORITE VACATION MEMORY:
Antique shopping on Portobello Road

BAD HABIT:
She can sometimes have a big head.

QUOTE:
"There's a fungus among us!"

****** JUICY ORANGE *******

LIKES:
Juicy secrets

DISLIKES:
Rhyming

KNOWN FOR:
Her pithy jokes

SPORTS SKILL:
The squeeze play

QUOTE:
"I'm juiced up and ready to go!"

******* CORNY COB *******

LIKES:
Puzzles and maizes

PRIZED POSSESSION:
Silk pajamas

SIGNATURE DANCE MOVE:
Pop and lock

FAVORITE COLOR:
Butter yellow

BEST FEATURE:
His husky voice

STRAWBERRY KISS

FAVORITE HOLIDAY:
Valentine's Day

BEST FRIEND:
Apple Blossom

FAVORITE SONG:
"Strawberry Fields Forever"

LIKES:
Pink lemonade

FAVORITE SINGER:
Berry Manilow

DREAMS ABOUT:
What's in the strawberry patch at the end of the rainbow

When Strawberry Kiss isn't lost in a daydream, you're sure to find her working on a new poem. Here's one she just finished! *Roses are red, violets are blue, Shopkins are sweet, and so are you!*

******* POSH PEAR *********

PERSONALITY:
Sweet, but a little spoiled

FAVORITE ANIMAL:
Partridge

PERFECT ACCESSORY:
Her pink "pear"
of sunglasses

BEST FRIEND:
Lippy Lips

QUOTE:
"I can't help it if
I have appeal."

**** PINEAPPLE CRUSH ****

BEST VACATION MEMORY:
A luau in Hawaii

CAN'T GET ENOUGH OF:
Fun in the sun

HOBBIES:
Sunbaking and hanging ten

FAVORITE WEATHER:
A tropical breeze

KNOWN FOR:
Her golden outlook on life

The Bakery aisle is always warm and inviting. These "well-bread" Shopkins make sure to savor the sweeter things in life.

BAKERY

****** D'LISH DONUT ******

FAVORITE SPORT:
Golf. She always gets a hole-in-one!

LOVES WHEN:
There's a light frosting of snow on the ground

HOBBY:
Glazing pottery

BEST FRIEND:
Cheeky Chocolate

BAD HABIT:
Frittering the day away

QUOTE:
"I dough-know what I'd do without my friends!"

****** MINI MUFFIN ******

FAVORITE MEAL:
Brunch

BEST TIME OF DAY:
Morning. She's an early riser!

SPORTS SKILL:
Yoga, especially the sunrise salutation

BEST FRIEND:
Spilt Milk

QUOTE:
"Today is a bran-new day!"

***** SLICK BREADSTICK ****

PERSONALITY:
Crusty on the outside,
but warm on the inside

FAVORITE HANGOUT:
A Parisian café

DISLIKES:
Rain. It makes him feel soggy.

BEST FRIENDS:
Alpha Soup and Fasta Pasta

QUOTE:

"Zer is always time for
ze café break, no?"

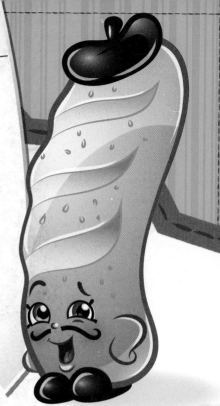

****** BREAD HEAD *******

LIKES:
Saving his dough

DISLIKES:
Stale jokes

FAVORITE ACCESSORY:
Loafers

GREATEST FEAR:
Getting sandwiched in a tight space

QUOTE:

"You're just buttering me up!"

FAVORITE COLORS:
Black and white

SPORTS SKILL:
Dunking

KNOWN FOR:
Milking a joke

GOOD AT:
Thinking outside the cookie jar

NICKNAME:
Snickerdoodle

SECRET TALENT:
Fortune-telling

QUOTE:
"My dad says I'm a chip off the old block!"

KOOKY COOKIE

Kooky Cookie may be shy and a little crumbly around the edges, but her friends know she's very well-rounded.

*** CARRIE CARROT CAKE ***

SIGNATURE DANCE MOVE:
Raisin' the roof

KNOWN FOR:
Getting to the root of a problem

PERSONALITY:
Sweet but a little nutty

PRIZED POSSESSION:
Her 14-carrot gold ring

QUOTE:
"As long as you have friends, everything else is just frosting."

**** MARY MERINGUE *****

KNOWN FOR:
Whipping up treats

BAD HABIT:
Her sweet tooth

PERSONALITY:
She always has her head in the clouds.

SECRET WEAPON:
A dollop of courage

HOMETOWN:
Born and baked in Alaska

AISLE 3
What's Cookin'?

The seasoned Shopkins in the Pantry aisle are full of flavor. But watch out! Some of them can be a bit wild and like to spice things up!

PANTRY

GRAN JAM

FAVORITE COLOR:
Raspberry pink

HOBBIES:
Knitting and jamming on the ukulele

SIGNATURE DANCE MOVE:
The jelly roll

KNOWN FOR:
Preserving memories in her scrapbook

HERO:
Alexander the Grape

BAD HABIT:
Stewing in her own juices

QUOTE:
"Aren't you a little sweetie?"

 This caring mama watches over all of Shopville. She spreads love and slathers affection on the Shopkins, sweetening their lives with her kind words.

☀☀☀☀☀☀ SALLY SHAKES ☀☀☀☀☀☀

HER FRIENDS SAY:
"Sally Shakes adds flavor to life!"

DISLIKES:
Unsavory characters

SPORTS SKILL:
The pinch hit

HOBBY:
Rock climbing

FAVORITE BAND:
The Spiced Girls

☀☀☀☀☀☀ PEPPE PEPPER ☀☀☀☀☀☀

KNOWS HOW TO:
Shake it on the dance floor

WISHES HE:
Could stop sneezing!

COUSINS:
Jalapeño, Cayenne, and Paprika

BEST FRIEND:
Sally Shakes.
They're rarely seen apart.

QUOTE:
"Let's spice things up!"

✳✳✳✳✳✳✳ HONEEEY ✳✳✳✳✳✳✳✳✳

HOBBIES:
The spelling bee and catching flies

GREATEST FEAR:
Getting hives

BEST FRIEND:
Lee Tea

LOVES TO:
Comb the pages of
a good magazine

QUOTE:
"What's the buzz?"

✳✳✳✳✳✳✳✳ FI FI FLOUR ✳✳✳✳✳✳✳✳

KNOWN FOR:
Being a bit of a mess

LIKES:
Half-baked ideas

DISLIKES:
Rolling pins and
feeling scattered

**FAVORITE
ACCESSORY:**
Her powder compact

QUOTE:
"Flour power!"

BREAKY CRUNCH

HOBBIES:
Bowling and staying in shape

LIKES:
Surprise gifts

DISLIKES:
Flakes

PERSONALITY:
He goes against the grain.

BEST FRIEND:
Spilt Milk

GREATEST FEAR:
Getting soggy

QUOTE:
"Nothing can box me up!"

Breaky Crunch wakes up at the crack of dawn each morning and heads to the gym. Lifting weights and getting in a few crunches is the perfect way to start his day!

***** SUGAR LUMP ****

PERSONALITY:
Sweet, but sometimes
a bit saccharine

LIKES:
Refined manners

SECRET TALENT:
Organization.
Storage cubes are her thing!

QUOTE:
"There's nothing sweeter
than friendship."

*** FASTA PASTA ***

FAVORITE ACCESSORY:
His bow tie

HOBBY:
Noodling around on the piano

PRIZED POSSESSION:
His lucky "penne"

SECRET WEAPON:
Elbow grease

****TOMMY KETCHUP ***

NICKNAME:
Squirt

LIKES:
Zesty debates

BEST FRIEND:
Frank Furter

QUOTE:
"Wait, guys! Let me catch up!"

AISLE 4
Cool and Creamy!

This is the aisle where everyone likes to chill out. All are welcome—the Dairy and Frozen Food Shopkins don't give anyone the cold shoulder!

DAIRY & FROZEN FOOD

KNOWN FOR:
Being a bit of a klutz

HOBBY:
Skimming through comic books

FAVORITE VACATION DESTINATION:
Wisconsin

PERSONALITY:
She cries over the little things.

FAVORITE WEATHER:
Pouring rain

DISLIKES:
Spoiled people really get her steamed!

BEST JOKE:
"What do you get from an Alaskan cow? *Ice cream!*"

SPILT MILK

You'll never be bored with Spilt Milk around! She's half silly and half serious, and really likes to stir things up!

✽✽✽✽✽✽✽✽ CHEE ZEE ✽✽✽✽✽✽✽✽

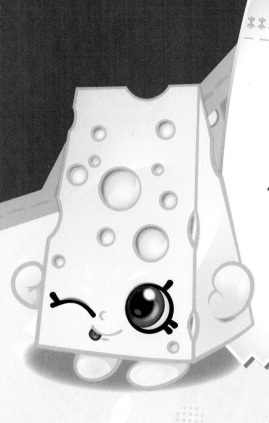

FAVORITE VACATION DESTINATION:
The Swiss Alps

BEST FRIENDS:
Freezy Peazy and Cheezey B

HIS FRIENDS SAY:
"Chee Zee can be a bit crackers."

FAVORITE SCARY BOOK:
Frankenstein's Muenster

QUOTE:
"Gouda been better.
Let's try it again!"

✽✽✽✽✽ FREEZY PEAZY ✽✽✽✽✽✽

FAVORITE WEATHER:
Snow

FIRST MEMORY:
Leaving the pod

PET PEEVE:
Bad manners.
He minds his p's and q's.

FAVORITE RAPPER:
Master P

******* POPSI COOL ********

LOVES TO:
Chill out

FUN FACT:
Rumor has it she has a twin.

HOBBIES:
Ice-skating and sledding

GREATEST FEAR:
Freezer burn

QUOTE:
"I can lick any problem!"

*********** YO-CHI **********

HOBBY:
Swirling around
the dance floor

**FAVORITE POP
MUSIC ARTIST:**
Vanilla Ice Cream

PERSONALITY:
Well-cultured

FASHION STYLE:
She's always sporting
a new topping.

QUOTE:
"Every day should have a
different flavor!"

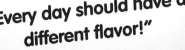

AISLE 5
It's Party Time!

There's always a reason to celebrate with these rockin' Shopkins. Whether it's someone's birthday or just an average Tuesday, they'll find something that deserves a special treat!

PARTY FOOD & SWEET TREATS

★★★★★★ LOLLI POPPINS ★★★★★★

PERSONALITY:
Sweet, but a little hard
to get along with

BAD HABIT:
She's stuck in her ways.

DISLIKES:
Lollygagging around

BEST FRIEND:
Candi Cotton

QUOTE:

"I'm no sucker!"

★★★★★★ BUBBLES ★★★★★★★★

LIKES:
A good chat-'n'-chew
with friends

KNOWN FOR:
Bursting into song

SPORTS SKILL:
Pop fly

BAD HABIT:
Flapping her gums

**FAVORITE MOVIE
CHARACTER:**
Chewbacca

STYLE SECRET:
Any color looks good on her.

BEST FRIEND:
Soda Pops

PERSONAL HERO:
Roy G. Biv

HOBBIES:
Painting

QUOTE:

"You need a little rain
to get a rainbow!"

****** SODA POPS ********

PERSONALITY:
Super-bubbly

DISLIKES:
Being shaken up

BAD HABIT:
Too much caffeine

HOBBY:
Refreshing her wardrobe

QUOTE:

"I hate to burst
your bubble . . ."

********* WISHES *********

AGE:
A year worth celebrating!

PRIZED POSSESSION:
Candles from her first birthday

FAVORITE SONG:
"When You Wish Upon a Star"

KNOWN FOR:
Throwing surprise parties

QUOTE:
"You *can* have your cake and eat it, too!"

******* WOBBLES *********

LIKES:
Wiggling to a good beat

FAVORITE SONG:
"Getting Jiggly With It"

PERSONALITY:
A worrier who bounces from problem to problem

PET PEEVE:
It feels like her friends can see right through her.

MOTTO:
Dancing shakes the stress away.

CHEEKY CHOCOLATE

BEST PRANK:
Convincing her friends she'd melted

BEST FRIENDS:
D'Lish Donut and Apple Blossom

FAVORITE ANIMAL:
Chocolate Labrador

FAVORITE VACATION DESTINATION:
Hershey, Pennsylvania

KNOWN FOR:
Breaking out laughing

HOBBIES:
Pulling pranks and melting hearts

QUOTE:
"Oops! I spilled the beans!"

Cheeky Chocolate loves to laugh. She's a prankster who isn't afraid of getting her hands dirty!

ICE CREAM DREAM **

BEST FRIEND:
Waffle Sue

PET PEEVE:
Brain freeze

PERSONALITY:
She can be a bit drippy.

NICKNAME:
Half-Pint

**** LE'QUORICE ******

PERSONALITY:
Some say she's an acquired taste.

HER FRIENDS KNOW:
She'll always stick by them.

FASHION STYLE:
Colorful layers

BEST FRIEND:
Mandy Candy

***** POPPY CORN ******

HOBBY:
Going to the movies

SPORTS SKILL:
None—he's a real butterfingers!

HAS A TENDENCY TO:
Pop up unexpectedly

QUOTE:
"I've got this in the bag!"

AISLE 6
Scrub-a-Dub!

The Cleaning and Laundry aisle is super fresh. The tidy Shopkins here make a game out of putting things in order. And they never play dirty!

CLEANING & LAUNDRY

Sparkle

SPORTS SKILL:
Mopping the floor with the competition

FAVORITE SONG:
"Whistle While You Work"

HER FRIENDS SAY:
"Molly can wring out any problem!"

KNOWN FOR:
Her strong work ethic

ENJOYS:
Checking things off her bucket list

LIKES:
Seeing her reflection in a clean, shiny floor

SECRET TALENT:
Getting a handle on the situation

MOLLY MOPS

 This hardworking miss knows how to get the job done. But don't be fooled by her can-do attitude—she's buckets of fun!

33

SIGNATURE DANCE MOVE:
The tootsie roll

LIKES TO:
Unwind with a good magazine

DISLIKES:
Feeling flushed

QUOTE:
"Let the good times roll!"

***** SQUEAKY CLEAN ******

PERSONALITY:
Honest and clean-cut

LIKES:
Water slides and bubble baths

DISLIKES:
Airing dirty laundry in public

BEST FRIEND:
Leafy

SECRET WEAPON:
The sparkle in his eye

QUOTE:
"Neat-o!"

AISLE 7
Home, Sweet Home!

Welcome to Aisle 7, where the friendly Baby and Homewares Shopkins are always eager for company! They're sure to make anyone feel right at home.

BABY & HOMEWARES

DUM MEE MEE

AGE:
Just a tyke

FAVORITE SINGER:
Lady Goo-Goo-Ga-Ga

FAVORITE COLOR:
Baby blue

SECRET TALENT:
Keeping the peace—she's a pacifier!

BEST FRIEND:
Sippy Sips

FAVORITE FLOWER:
Baby's breath

QUOTE:
"You'll never cry when I'm around."

 Dum Mee Mee is a little cutie who was born to shop. She may be tiny, but she's got a very big heart.

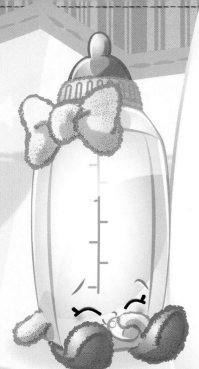

******** DRIBBLES ********

PERSONALITY:
She can be
rather formulaic.

RELAXES BY:
Reheating in a nice,
warm bath

LIKES:
Nursery rhymes

DISLIKES:
People who bottle
up their emotions

LOOKS UP TO:
Sippy Sips

****** SIPPY SIPS ********

KNOWN FOR:
Never spilling a secret

**FAVORITE
SPORTING EVENT:**
The World Cup

ENJOYS:
Singing lullabies before bedtime

PRIZED POSSESSION:
A stuffed bear

QUOTE:

"Enjoy life one sip at a time."

******* LANA LAMP *******

FAVORITE TIME OF DAY:
Bright and early

BEST FEATURE:
Her smile has serious wattage.

PERSONALITY:
Brilliant

KNOWN FOR:
Always looking on the bright side

QUOTE:
"We've got it made
in the shade!"

*** BRENDA BLENDER ****

LIKES:
Stirring up trouble

DISLIKES:
Blending in

PERSONALITY:
She's a real smoothie operator!

DREAMS ABOUT:
Having superpowers

QUOTE:
"Let's mix it up!"

TOASTY POP

HOBBIES:
Throwing parties and giving toasts

KNOWN FOR:
Never having a stale idea

DISLIKES:
Burning out

ISN'T AFRAID:
To grab a slice of life

BEST FRIEND:
Buttercup

FAVORITE WEATHER:
Dry heat

QUOTE:
"Let's get cookin'!"

 The only things warmer than Toasty Pop's personality are her words. When she gives a speech, there isn't a dry eye in the house.

The Shopkins in the Shoes and Fashion aisle are a always on the go! You can catch them kicking up dust as they sprint all over Small Mart, but at the end of the day they enjoy hanging out in pairs most

SHOES & FASHION

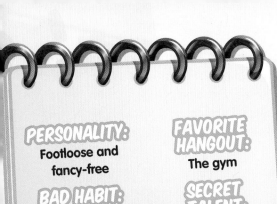

SNEAKY WEDGE

PERSONALITY:
Footloose and fancy-free

BAD HABIT:
Lying about his height

FAVORITE SPORT:
Marathons

FAVORITE HANGOUT:
The gym

SECRET TALENT:
He can be very sneaky.

QUOTE:
"I've got sole!"

Sneaky is known for being a bit mischievous, but don't let that fool you. He also has a straight-laced, go-getter side. When he puts his mind to something, he's sure to hit the ground running!

***** BUN BUN SLIPPER ****

SIGNATURE DANCE MOVE:
The bunny hop

PRIZED POSSESSION:
Lucky rabbit's foot

PERFECT ACCESSORY:
Her cozy bathrobe

PERSONAL HERO:
The Easter Bunny

QUOTE:

"I'll go toe-to-toe
with anyone!"

******** PROMMY *********

LIKES:
Getting dressed up
for special occasions

PERSONALITY:
High-spirited, never flat

KNOWN FOR:
Her fabulous style sense

HOBBY:
Kicking up her heels

QUOTE:

"You can never look
too gorgeous!"

AISLE 9
Lookin' Good!

The Health and Beauty aisle is the place to be when you want to look—and feel!—good. The Shopkins here are always polished, but they know true beauty is found on the inside.

HEALTH & BEAUTY

******* POLLY POLISH *******

PERSONALITY:
A risk-taker

STYLE SENSE:
She loves trying new colors.

KNOWN FOR:
Telling the unvarnished truth

DISLIKES:
Chips

QUOTE:

"Nailed it!"

******* SCRUBS *********

BEST FEATURE:
His pearly-white smile

PRIZED POSSESSION:
A golden toothbrush

FAVORITE COLOR:
Mint green

FAVORITE STORYBOOK CHARACTER:
The Cheshire Cat

QUOTE:

"Keep on smiling!"

********* SHAMPY *********

PERSONALITY:
Bubbly and stylish

BAD HABIT:
Getting worked up into a lather

FAVORITE WEATHER:
Rain showers

BEST FEATURE:
She always smells fresh.

SIGNATURE DANCE MOVE:
The wave

********* SILKY *********

PERSONALITY:
A smooth operator

PET PEEVE:
A bad hair day

DISLIKES:
Hot weather.
It makes her feel frizzy.

BEST FRIEND:
Shampy

LOVES:
Swimming and day spas

LIPPY LIPS

PERSONALITY:
Sassy and
a bit bossy

STYLE SENSE:
She has a different
shade for every mood

BEST FRIENDS:
Apple Blossom and
Polly Polish

LIKES:
Glossy magazines

DISLIKES:
Dull colors

HOBBIES:
Acting and
shopping

QUOTE:
"Have a
beautiful day!"

 There's one word to describe this fashionista: *beautiful*. Lippy Lips lives to shop, loves to gab, and leaves her mark wherever she goes!

Check them out before they fly off the shelf! The Shopkins in the Limited Edition aisle are only in Small Mart for a short time, and they make every second count!

LIMITED EDITION

KNOWN FOR:
His concentration

FAVORITE COLOR:
Citron

BEST FRIEND:
Sour Lemon

FAVORITE VACATION DESTINATION:
The Florida Keys

QUOTE:
"Pucker up!"

****** PAPA TOMATO *****

FAVORITE PASTIME:
Chatting with pals on the vine

AGE:
Let's just say he's ripe!

PRIZED POSSESSION:
Family heirlooms

KNOWN FOR:
Being a seasoned storyteller

BEST FRIEND:
Gran Jam

****** DONNA DONUT ******

HOBBY:
Holing up with a good book

FAVORITE WEATHER:
A sprinkle of rain

KNOWN FOR:
Having dozens of friends

FIRST MEMORY:
Popping out of the oven

FAVORITE SONG:
"Dough-Re-Mi"

******** LEE TEA *********

LIKES:
Handbags, shoulder bags, and tea bags!

DISLIKES:
Steep prices

FAVORITE ANIMAL:
Teacup pig

FAVORITE COLORS:
Black and green

QUOTE:
"I smell trouble brewing!"

*** TWINKY WINKS ****

PERSONALITY:
She's full of surprises.

BAD HABIT:
Sponging off her friends

DISLIKES:
Needing fillings
at the dentist

QUOTE:
"Shopkins are the
cream of the crop!"

*** MARSHA MELLOW ***

HER FRIENDS SAY:
"She's a real softie!"

BEST FRIEND:
Choco Lava

LOVES TO:
Tell stories by
the campfire

QUOTE:
"Let's play s'more!"

*** CUPCAKE QUEEN ***

ENJOYS:
Hosting grand balls

FAVORITE ACCESSORY:
A crown of frosting

PRIZED POSSESSION:
Red-velvet slippers

DREAMS ABOUT:
Becoming royalty

FAVORITE VACATION DESTINATION:
Miami Beach

PERFECT ACCESSORY:
Her sunglasses, of course

FAVORITE WEATHER:
The hotter the better!

FAVORITE COLOR:
Ultraviolet

ENJOYS:
A coconut-banana smoothie

QUOTE:
"Life is a day at the beach!"

SPF 30+

Sunny Screen can be a bit of a worrier, but deep down she just wants to take care of her friends. No one's getting burned on her watch!

****** TIN'A'TUNA ******

FAVORITE SONG:
"Roe, Roe, Roe Your Boat"

LIKES:
Swimming upstream

DISLIKES:
Canned applause

FAVORITE CHARACTER:
The Tin Man

QUOTE:
"Something's fishy!"

******* BUTTERCUP *******

SECRET TALENT:
He has great taste!

FIRST MEMORY:
Being whipped into shape

FAVORITE COLOR:
Mellow yellow

PERSONALITY:
Rich, but never spoiled

HIS FRIENDS SAY:
"Buttercup will melt
your heart!"

**** ANGIE ANKLE BOOT ****

NICKNAME:
Tootsie

KNOWN FOR:
Taking problems in stride

PERSONALITY:
Practical, yet sleek

FAVORITE ACCESSORY:
Leg warmers

QUOTE:
"Don't go getting too big for your boots!"

***** RUB-A-GLOVE *******

KNOWN FOR:
Dishing the dirt

HOBBY:
Water sports

BEST FRIEND:
Molly Mops

PRIZED POSSESSION:
Her rubber duck

QUOTE:
"Can you give me a hand?"

COLLECTOR'S SHOPPING LIST

CHECK OFF YOUR COLLECTED SHOPKINS TO SEE WHICH ONES YOU STILL HAVE TO FIND!

- ○ COMMON
- RARE
- ● ULTRA RARE
- SPECIAL EDITION

FINISHES:

 GLITTER SHOPKINS

 FROZEN SHOPKINS

 METALLIC SHOPKINS

 BLING SHOPKINS

FLUFFY BABY SHOPKINS

There are so many Shopkins to check out. Use this list to collect the whole bunch!

SEASON 1
✱✱✱✱✱✱ FRUIT & VEG ✱✱✱✱✱✱

Apple Blossom 1-001 ○	Rockin' Broc 1-002 ○	Strawberry Kiss 1-003 ○	Pineaple Crush 1-004 ○
Melonie Pips 1-005 ●	Miss Mushy-Moo 1-006 ○	Posh Pear 1-007 ○	Apple Blossom 2-008 ○
Rockin' Broc 1-009 ○	Strawberry Kiss 1-010 ○	Pineapple Crush 1-011 ○	Melonie Pips 1-012 ●
Miss Musshy-Moo 1-013 ○	Posh Pear 1-014 ○		

SEASON 2
✱✱✱✱✱✱ FRUIT & VEG ✱✱✱✱✱✱

Chloe Flower 2-001 ○	Sour Lemon 2-002 ●	Juicy Orange 2-003 ○	Corny Cob 2-004 ○
Garlic Rose 2-005 ○	Boo-Hoo Onion 2-006 ○	Dippy Avocado 2-007 ○	Silly Chilli 2-008 ○
Chloe Flower 2-009 ○	Sour Lemon 2-010 ●	Juicy Orange 2-011 ○	Corny Cob 2-012 ●
Garlic Rose 2-013 ○	Boo-Hoo Onion 2-014 ○	Dippy Avocado 2-015 ○	Silly Chilli 2-016 ○

****** BAKERY ******

Bread Head 1-033  ○	Creamy Bun-Bun 1-034 ○	D'lish Donut 1-035 ●	Cheese Kate 1-036 ○
Mini Muffin 1-037 ○	Flutter Cake 1-038 ○	Kookie Cookie 1-039 ●	Bread Head 1-040 ○
Creamy Bun-Bun 1-041 ○	D'lish Donut 1-042 ●	Cheese Kate 1-043 ○	Mini Muffin 1-044 ○
Flutter Cake 1-045 ○	Kookie Cookie 1-046 ●		

******* BAKERY *******

Slick Breadstick 2-035 ○	Mary Muffin 2-036 ●	Carrie Carrot Cake 2-037 ○	Mary Meringue 2-038 ●
Pecanna Pie 2-039 ○	Choco Lava 2-040 ○	Fifi Fruit Tart 2-041 ○	Danni Danish 2-042 ○
Cupcake Chic 2-043 ○	Slick Breadstick 2-044 ○	Mary Muffin 2-045 ●	Carrie Carrot Cake 2-046 ○
Mary Meringue 2-047 ●	Pecanna Pie 2-048 ○	Choco Lava 2-049 ○	Fifi Fruit Tart 2-050 ○
Danni Danish 2-051 ○	Cupcake Chic 2-052 ○		

SEASON 1
PANTRY

Tommy Ketchup 1-015 ○	Nutty Butter 1-016 ◐	Peppe Pepper 1-017 ○	Sally Shakes 1-018 ◐
Sugar Lump 1-019 ●	Breaky Crunch 1-020 ●	Alpha Soup 1-021 ○	Gran Jam 1-022 ○
Coolio 1-023 ○	Tommy Ketchup 1-024 ○	Nutty Butter 1-025 ○	Peppe Pepper 1-026 ○
Sally Shakes 1-027 ◐	Sugar Lump 1-028 ●	Breaky Crunch 1-029 ●	Alpha Soup 1-030 ○
Gran Jam 1-031 ○	Coolio 1-032 ○		

SEASON 2
PANTRY

Fi Fi Flour 2-069 ○	Bart Beans 2-070 ○	Fasta Pasta 2-071 ○	Olivia Oil 2-072 ●
Honeeey 2-073 ●	Al Foil 2-074 ○	Toffy Coffee 2-075 ○	Cornell Mustard 2-076 ○
Chris P Crackers 2-077 ○	Fi Fi Flour 2-078 ○	Bart Beans 2-079 ○	Fasta Pasta 2-080 ○
Olivia Oil 2-081 ●	Honeeey 2-082 ○	Al Foil 2-083 ●	Toffy Coffee 2-084 ○
Cornell Mustard 2-085 ○	Chris P Crackers 2-086 ◐		

57

:::::::::SEASON 1:::::::::
******* DAIRY *******

Chee Zee 1-065	Swiss Miss 1-066	Spilt Milk 1-067	Ghurty 1-068
○	○	⬤	○

Millie Shake 1-069	Flava Ava 1-070	Dollops 1-071	Googy 1-072
⬤	○	○	○

Chee Zee 1-073	Swiss Miss 1-074	Spilt Milk 1-075	Ghurty 1-076
○	○	○	○

Millie Shake 1-077	Flava Ava 1-078	Dollops 1-079	Googy 1-080
⬤	○	○	○

:::::::::SEASON 1:::::::::
******** FROZEN ********

Ice Cream Dream 1-121	Popsi Cool 1-122	Yo-Chi 1-123	Cool Cube 1-124
○	○	○	○

Pa' Pizza 1-125	Snow Crush 1-126	Fishtix 1-127	Freezy Peazy 1-128
○	○	○	○

Ice Cream Dream 1-129	Popsi Cool 1-130	Yo-Chi 1-131	Cool Cube 1-132
○	○	○	○

Pa' Pizza 1-133	Snow Crush 1-134	Fishtix 1-135	Freezy Peazy 1-136
○	○	○	○

SEASON 1
***** SWEET TREATS *****

Bubbles
1-047

Candy
Kisses
1-048

Le'Quorice
1-049

Cheeky
Chocolate
1-050

Candi
Cotton
1-051

Lolli
Poppins
1-052

Mandy
Candy
1-053

Jelly B
1-054

Miss
Twist
1-055

Bubbles
1-056

Candy
Kisses
1-057

Le'Quorice
1-058

Cheeky
Chocolate
1-059

Candi
Cotton
1-060

Lolli
Poppins
1-061

Mandy
Candy
1-062

Jelly B
1-063

Miss
Twist
1-064

SEASON 2
SWEET TREATS *****

Poppy
Corn
2-053

Minnie
Mintie
2-054

Banana
Splitty
2-055

Yummy
Gum
2-056

Waffle
Sue
2-057

Ice Cream
Dream
2-058

Cheery
Churro
2-059

Pamela
Pancake
2-060

Poppy
Corn
2-061

Minnie
Mintie
2-062

Banana
Splitty
2-063

Yummy
Gum
2-064

Waffle
Sue
2-065

Ice Cream
Dream
2-066

Cheery
Churro
2-067

Pamela
Pancake
2-068

SEASON 2
✳✳✳ CLEANING & LAUNDRY ✳✳✳

Dishy Liquid 2-087	Squeaky Clean 2-088	Wendy Washer 2-089	Bree Freshner 2-090
Molly Mops 2-091	Sweeps 2-092	Sarah Softner 2-093	Peta Plunger 2-094
Leafy 2-095	Dishy Liquid 2-096	Squeaky Clean 2-097	Wendy Washer 2-098
Bree Freshner 2-099	Molly Mops 2-100	Sweeps 2-101	Sarah Softner 2-102
	Peta Plunger 2-103	Leafy 2-104	

SEASON 2
✳✳✳✳✳✳✳✳ BABY ✳✳✳✳✳✳✳✳

Dribbles 2-121	Ga Ga Gourmet 2-122	Dum Mee Mee 2-123	Baby Swipes 2-124
Sippy Sips 2-125	Baby Puff 2-126	Nappy Dee 2-127	Shampoo Sue 2-128
Dribbles 2-129	Ga Ga Gourmet 2-130	Dum Mee Mee 2-131	Baby Swipes 2-132
Sippy Sips 2-133	Baby Puff 2-134	Nappy Dee 2-135	Shampoo Sue 2-136

SEASON 2 :::::::
****** HOMEWARES *****

Toasty Pop 2-017 ○	Brenda Blender 2-018 ●	Coffee Drip 2-019 ○	Saucy Pan 2-020 ●
Ma Kettle 2-021 ○	Zappy Microwave 2-022 ●	Lisa Litter 2-023 ○	Lana Lamp 2-024 ●
Sizzles 2-025 ○	Toasty Pop 2-026 ○	Brenda Blender 2-027 ○	Coffee Drip 2-028 ○
Saucy Pan 2-029 ○	Ma Kettle 2-030 ○	Zappy Microwave 2-031 ●	Lisa Litter 2-032 ○
Lana Lamp 2-033 ●	Sizzles 2-034 ○		

:::::::: SEASON 2 ::::::
****** SHOES ******

Prommy 2-105 ○	Sneaky Sue 2-106 ●	Heels 2-107 ○	Sneaky Wedge 2-108 ○
Betty Boot 2-109 ○	Wedgy Wendy 2-110 ○	Bun Bun Slipper 2-111 ○	Cute Boot 2-112 ●
Prommy 2-113 ○	Sneaky Sue 2-114 ○	Heels 2-115 ○	Sneaky Wedge 2-116 ○
Betty Boot 2-117 ○	Wedgy Wendy 2-118 ○	Bun Bun Slipper 2-119 ○	Cute Boot 2-120 ●

SEASON 1
*** HEALTH & BEAUTY ***

Scrubs 1-101	Lippy Lips 1-102	Curly 1-103	Shampy 1-104
Silky 1-105	Bubble Tubs 1-106	Chap-Elli 1-107	Polly Polish 1-108
Suds 1-109	Toofs 1-110	Scrubs 1-111	Lippy Lips 1-112
Curly 1-113	Shampy 1-114	Silky 1-115	Bubble Tubs 1-116
Chap-Elli 1-117	Polly Polish 1-118	Subs 1-119	Toofs 1-120

:::::: SEASON 1 ::::::
★★★★★ **LIMITED EDITION** ★★★★★

Cupcake Queen 1-137

Buttercup 1-138

Tin'a' Tuna 1-139

Twinky Winks 1-140

Papa Tomato 1-141

Sunny Screen 1-142

:::::: SEASON 2 ::::::
★★★★★ **LIMITED EDITION** ★★★★★

Marsha Mellow 2-137

Rub-a-Glove 2-138

Lenny Lime 2-139

Lee Tea 2-140

Donna Donut 2-141

Angie Ankle Boot 2-142